Peter thought,
"Those feathers would make
my arrows fly better."

So he pulled the feathers
off the hat, and his bubble gum
stuck to the brim.

But Mrs Honey didn't notice.

Mrs Honey's Hat

written and illustrated
by Pam Adams

Child's Play®

Mrs Honey had a hat.

On Monday,
she wore it when she took
her grandson Peter to the park.
She bought him
some bubble gum
and sat on a bench
with her knitting.

On Tuesday,
Mrs Honey wore her hat
to visit a friend.

They sat in the garden
in the shade of a tree
and ate cakes.

Some birds flew down
to pick up the crumbs.
"Those cherries look good,"
they chirped.

So they flew off with them.
One little bird left
some eggs behind.

But Mrs Honey didn't notice.

On Wednesday,
Mrs Honey spent a day
at the seaside.

The sun shone, and the water
was just right for paddling.
Mrs Honey felt very happy.

Afterwards, Mrs Honey
took off her hat
and sat in the sun.
A hermit crab thought,
"That shell would make
a nice new home."

So he scuttled away
with the shell, and left
some seaweed behind.

But Mrs Honey didn't notice.

On Thursday,
Mrs Honey picked
dandelions to make wine.

It was very hard work.
She took off her hat
and put it on the fence.

A cow in the field
saw the hat on the fence.
"What beautiful big buttercups,"
she mooed.

So she took a mouthful,
and her bell fell
onto Mrs Honey's hat.

But Mrs Honey didn't notice.

On Friday,
Mrs Honey went
to see an old castle.
"Just look at those cobwebs,"
exclaimed Mrs Honey.
"This place could do
with a good clean!"

A big, black spider
dropped onto her hat.
"Hurrah!" he said.
"This lace will make
a good strong cobweb."

So he hurried away
with the lace, and left
all his old webs behind.

But Mrs Honey didn't notice.

On Saturday,
Mrs Honey took her cat
to a cat show.
There were all sorts
of fine cats, but she hoped
that hers would win first prize.

An alley cat
saw Mrs Honey's hat
through the window.
"That ribbon might help me
to win first prize," he thought.

So he pulled it from the hat
and left some fish bones behind.

But Mrs Honey didn't notice.

On Sunday,
Mrs Honey went to church.
Everyone seemed
to be staring at her.
"Whatever can it be?"
she wondered.
"Perhaps it's time
I bought a new hat."

After the service,
Mrs Honey hurried home
to look in the mirror.
Then she noticed
the bubble gum, the eggs,
the seaweed, the bell,
the cobwebs and the fish bones.
"Goodness," she exclaimed.
"I've **got** a new hat!"

But she wasn't sure that she liked it!

Monday Tuesday Wednesday

Do you remember what happened to Mrs Honey's hat?
On each day of the week, one item was replaced
with another. Can you match them with each day?

Ribbon

Fish Bones

Buttercups

Cherries

Shell

Thursday   Friday   Saturday

Cobwebs

Lace

Feathers

Eggs

Bell

Bubble Gum

Seaweed

Sunday

"I've **got** a new hat!"